SKIPPYS
A HERO NOW

FUGITIVE KIND

Johnny Arbogast

SKIPPYS A HERO NOW

Santa Cruz   ~   San Francisco

ISBN 978-0-578-06946-3

FUGITIVE KIND

PREFACE

FUGITIVE KIND is based on three short stories I wrote while at Emerson College in Boston, just before my son was born in 1992. They were: "Collision", "Hits and Misses", and "Breakfast at Tiffany's". I decided that a screenplay was the best format for telling this story, and it is really less a screenplay than a very cinematically structured poem. The title and epigraph are cribbed from the song "Fugitive Kind", by Paul Westerberg, which I would recommend the reader listen to as they begin to read this.

There were many people who helped me along the way in various manners. I am grateful to each of them and they are listed here alphabetically by their unnamed surname: Campbell, Jody, Davey Baby, Brandon, Christine, Lisa, George, Darcy, Ari, Amy, Freddie, Betsy, Dave and Donna, Samantha and Steve.

Thanks, guys.

Johnny Arbogast
September 2010
Felton, California

I'm a bad idea whose time has come,
And I'll never forget where I started from.
I'm the fugitive kind,
You better make up your mind,
I can't wait.

~ Paul Westerberg

CAST

Reily

Bartender

School Administrator 1

School Administrator 2

School Administrator 3

Tom/Tommy

Michelle/Shelley

Dog Walker 1

Dog Walker 2

Jeff

Lily

Charles

Intercom Monica

First

Second

Tiffany

Cousin

Mike

Twins

Bookstore Employee

INT. BAR – EARLY EVENING

Inside a small, local bar. The bar itself is off to the right and run the length of the room. Two guys are at the near end, drinking beers from bottles and watching Sports Center on ESPN on the TV behind the bar, they are really into it, frequently questioning each other as to whether the other had just seen the last highlight.

The bartender, solid looking gut in his 50's with an iron grey crew cut, is leaning back reading a newspaper about halfway down the bar.

CUT TO:
EXT. BAR – THE SUN IS SETTNG

Reily walks down the sidewalk towards the bar, his hands in the pockets of his jacket. He's dejected looking but not walking slowly. He walks up to the door of the bar and pulls open the door.

CUT TO:
INT BAR – EARLY EVENING

A bell rings as the door opens and the bartender looks up to see who has come in. A look of recognition, mixed with pity and disgust crosses his face and ends in bored contempt. He goes back to reading his paper.

                    REILY
            Good evening Adam!

The bartender, whose name isn't Adam, doesn't look up, in fact doesn't say anything for a moment, then, never looking up from his paper:

BARTENDER
Take it easy tonight Reily, I'm in no fucking mood.

Reily lifts both his hands, palms out, as he continues to walk toward the bar.

REILY
I assure you, Arthur, that I will be the soul of discretion, a veritable bastion of decorum and gentlemanly behavior.

The bartender stares at him again with naked contempt before ignoring him and going back to reading his paper.

Reily sits at one of the stools in the middle of the bar, three or four stools down from the other two guys. He unbuttons his jacket and pulls his wallet from his inside jacket pocket. He plucsk out a twenty, which seems to empty his wallet, and lays it on the bar.

The bartender still does not look up from his paper.

BARTENDER
What's it gonna be?

REILY
I think tonight... Hmmm... I've been a little rundown lately, probably fighting off something, cold and 'flu season, you know, hmmm, let's see...

Reily puts a finger to his lips in contemplation.

The bartender closes his paper roughly, setting it on the counter behind him.

                    BARTENDER
          Oh, for fuck's sake...
He starts to walk away from Reily, toward the back of the bar.

                    REILY
                 (Quickly)
          Let's make it a Cuervo and grapefruit juice, please, on
          the rocks if you would.

The bartender grimaces, as though he can't imagine drinking something like that, then without even really trying, he sloshes a shot of tequila into a glass of ice and pours juice from a plastic pitcher that was tucked away somewhere under the bar.

He sets Reily's drink on the bar, then walks down to the other two guys, swooping up two longneck beer bottles on his way and uncapping both before he gets to them. He sets them on the bar; backing up the two they are already drinking.

                    BARTENDER
          These are on Reily, guys.

The two look up from their conversation and each lifts his bottle in a salute of thanks.

Reily looks down at them, somewhat dismayed, he obviously had no idea he was going to be buying the house a round.

The bartender comes back and makes the twenty disappear. The cash register rings once and the drawer shoots open. He turns back and sets some bills in front of Reily.

REILY
(Frowning a little)

Thanks.

BARTENDER

Maybe that'll slow you down a little.

REILY

I'm really in no position...

BARTENDER

Shuddup, you got a job, you make good dough, those two guys've been laid off four months now, have a heart would ya, Reily.

CUT TO:
INT. CONFERENCE ROOM, A POSH ELEMENTARY SCHOOL – DAY

Reilly sits in a chair facing a long table. On the other side of the table are four serious looking administrators looking at him. Reily looks a little disheveled and there are small flecks of colorful clay stuck to his clothes.

CUT TO:
CU

SCHOOL ADMINISTRATOR 1

> Mr. Reily, in light of this situation as well as others of
> a similar nature going back over your fourteen months
> with this educational institution...

CUT TO:
CU

> SCHOOL ADMINISTRATOR 2
> For God's sake Reily, several of the children required
> medical attention, parents had to be called, and we'll
> all be lucky if the school isn't sued...

CUT TO:
CU

> SCHOOL ADMINISTRATOR 1
> ... We really have no choice but to ask you for your
> resignation...

CUT TO:
CU

> SCHOOL ADMINISTRATOR 3
> God knows you are no teacher.

CUT TO:
*Reily's shoulders slump slightly at hearing this. He looks down at
the floor and gives a long sigh.*

> SCHOOL ADMINISTRATOR 1
> ... Effective immediately.

*The administrator picks up his sheaf of files and papers and,
standing them up, begins to tap them against the table to
straighten them. He looks to his left and murmurs something to*

one of the other administrators who chuckles a little. They are all completely ignoring him now.

CUT TO:

INT. CLASSROOM – MORNING

[SILENT SCENE, MUSIC ONLY]

There are about 25 kids in the classroom, and Reily, in his element, excited and possibly, visibly intoxicated on something. His eyes are wild and happy, and he is pointing in several different directions at the same time. The children are moving chaotically, apparently laughing and chatting with each other, as they clear all the desk and chairs off to the side. Reily issues another instruction once the room is clear, his stance wavering slightly when he stands still, and a majority of the children line up against an empty wall. They all close their eyes tight with their hands clasped in front of them.

At the back of the classroom, Reily and four or five students carry large containers that appear fairly heavy, the smaller students struggling to carry them to a table about fifteen feet from the wall where the students are lined up.

CUT TO:

INT. BAR – EARLY EVENING

In the back of the bar, looking along it towards the front door. Reily sips his drink slowly, before reaching into his jacket for a pack of cigarettes and matches. He puts one to his lips and lights it with a match, then somewhat theatrically shaking out the match in long slow waves.

The bartender, who had been at the other end wiping down part of the bar, sidles up the bar and as the match goes out –

CUT TO:

EXTREME CU

Reily's hand waving the match, immediately slow motion to barely moving, the match goes out and a small trail of smoke winds upward.

CUT TO:

EXTREME CU

The surface of the bar is smacked with the meaty hand of the bartender, the sound is of something solid though, and when he lifts his hand there is a cheap glass ashtray.

REILY

Thank you, Atticus.

Drops the burnt match and takes a sip of his drink.

And how are matters with you today?

BARTENDER

You know what your problem is Reily? You're too fuckin' smart for your own good. You never say one word when you can make it three, and you don't talk like a normal person anyway, and to top it off you are one seriously fucked up dipshit. Now, will you quit callin' me those fuckin' names, you want to know my name then ask like a normal person.

REILY

(Looking vaguely weary as if he's been through this before)

Okay, what's your name?

BARTENDER

None a your fuckin' business; now you want another
drink or what? Those boys down there are thirsty
tonight.

*Reily picks up the small pile of bills and fans them out so he can
count.*

CUT TO:
EXTREME CU
The money on the bar, fanned out by Reily, a ten and three singles.

CUT TO:
*Reily looking at the bills and his drink, which is less than a quarter
full, mostly ice and water.*

REILY

I'm content for the moment, Alvin, remember, you said
go easy tonight.

*The bartender looks at him for a long pause, deciding what to say,
and possibly even what to feel, and then he turns and walks back
toward the back of the bar and vanishes into a back-storage area.*

*Reily watches him walk away, then downs the rest of his drink and
slides off the stool and heads for the men's room off to the left of
where the bartender has exited. He pulls open the door.*

CUT TO:
INT. THE BAR'S MEN'S ROOM

Reily enters and catches sight of himself in the bathroom mirror.
He reaches a hand up to touch a spot of bright blue in his hair.

The buzzing of the fluorescent light becomes louder as Reily
stares at himself in the mirror, the sound changes to a faint echoic
sound of children first laughing then mingling with some screams.

CUT TO:
EXTREME CU
Reily's reflection, there are numerous flecks of brightly colored
specks in his hair and on his neck and collar.

His hand moves in slow motion to the laughing-screaming,
touching the color spots, lost in reverie.

The sound gradually transitions back to the buzzing light.

CUT TO:

Reily standing in front of the mirror, he shakes his head as if to
shake away bad thoughts and turns and opens the door of the
single stall.

CUT TO:
INT. BATHROOM STALL

Reily reaches out and puts the cracked partial toilet seat down,
then sits down and takes a deep breath. He reaches into his inside
jacket pocket and takes a thin plastic case, such as one would

keep small fishing lures in. He opens it to reveal pills in a variety of shapes and colors.

CUT TO:
EXTREME CU

All the pills fill the frame.

CUT TO:
EXTREME CU

Reily's face, which has taken on an air of calm.

CUT TO:
EXTREME CU

The pills fill the frame, slowly beginning to revolve, then faster and faster, as the pills dissolve into a swirl of colors, the buzz of the lights once again becomes children laughing and screaming, the colors continue to swirl.

CUT TO:
INT. CLASSROOM – DAYTIME

There is the same laughter and screaming of children, but not synched with the scene unfolding which is silent. Reily, almost stumbling, digs one hand into a large container and brings out what looks like bright blue soupy mud. He holds it above the container for a moment and seems to be lecturing the gathered children. All of a sudden he turns and hurls the handful at the children lined up against the wall.

CUT TO:
CU

The line of children against the wall which is already streaked with blue. A handful of red is thrown, then one of green.

CUT TO:
INT. BATHROOM STALL
EXTREME CU

All the pills fill the frame, Reily's fingers enter and pluck one of the large red pills then another, and one of the green one.

CUT TO:

Reily, having made his selections, puts the pill case back in his breast pocket and stands up to leave the stall. He walks over to the sink, and just as he's reaching to turn on the water, again catches his own eye in the mirror.

CUT TO:
INT. REILY'S APARTMENT BATHROOM – THAT MORNING

Reily is facing the mirror in his bathroom, whistling as he ties his necktie. He looks freshly shave and groomed. He tugs the knot tight and the fusses with it, tightening and straightening. Finishing, he looks at it for a moment, examining how it looks in the mirror. He leaves the bathroom and walks through his very cramped apartment to the kitchen. On the kitchen table is the same pill case, next to a full glass and a carton of orange juice. There is a small TV in the background with a news anchor speaking; the volume is too low to hear what's being said. Reily looks at a digital clock on the stove which reads 7:10

CUT TO:
EXTREME CU

Reily's hand with several different colored pills in it, in slow motion the hand starts to slightly shake and the pills jostle back and forth.

CUT TO:
INT-REILY'S APARTMENT KITCHEN – MORNING
Reily standing in the kitchen throws his head back and tosses all the pills into his mouth. He reaches for the glass of orange juice and takes a large gulp to wash down the pills, swallowing several times, then drinks down the rest.

CUT TO:
EXTREME CU
Reily's hand setting the juice glass in the sink. The click of glass hitting the sink echoes.

CUT TO:
EXT. REILY'S APRATMENT BUILDING – MORNING
The door opens and Reily comes out, he is carrying a briefcase. There are people moving here and there, on their way to work. The occasional car drifts past, it is not a very busy street. Reily pauses at the top of the steps and seems to consider the air before descending the steps.

Once on the sidewalk Reily begins to walk down the block.

CUT TO:

INT. SMALL DELI – MORNING

Reily stands at the counter in line, waiting to buy a cup of coffee. He is starting to sway slightly and as he stands still he zones out periodically for a second or two before snapping back. It is silent inside the deli except for the sound of being deep underwater.

GUY BEHIND THE COUNTER

[OFF SCREEN, FAINT, FAR AWAY]
What's it going to be pal?

The guy behind the counter reaches across and snaps his fingers a few times in front of Reily.

All of a sudden the deli sounds are all there, multiple people talking, the sounds of milk being steamed, and a radio morning show in the background.

REILY

Excuse me, Baxter (the guy's nametag reads Fred). Uh, a large coffee, regular, please. (*Remembers and slaps his jacket pocket*). And a pack of Chesterfield's too.

GUY BEHIND THE COUNTER

$5.75.

He takes Reily's proffered bill, rings the register and slaps the change down and looks over Reily's shoulder to the customer behind.

Next! What can I get you?

CUT TO:
INT. CLASSROOM – MORNING

Reily enters the classroom, carrying his coffee and briefcase, as he closes the door behind him, all the ambient noise of the school hallways is shut off too. He walks over to the far back corner and sets his briefcase on the floor and his coffee on the desk. He sits down at the desk and stares out the window.

CUT TO:
EXT. OUTSIDE CLASSROOM WINDOW – MORNING

Out the window there are people walking and cars driving. Everything moves faster then slower then faster then slower again. The only sound is deep underwater.

CUT TO:
INT. CLASSROOM – MORNING

(A bell rings) The door to Reily's classroom opens and a stream of fourth-graders flows in and begin sitting at the desks, chattering and laughing.

CUT TO:
Reily sits at the back of the room with his feet on his desk. (Another bell rings) The second bell jolts him out of his reverie and the children fall silent. Reily stands slowly and unsteadily then makes his way to the front of the room.

REILY

Good morning, ladies and gentlemen.

                    CHILDREN
            (All at once but not in unison)
    Good morning, Mr. Reily.

                     REILY
How would you all like to do something really
interesting today? A group-project, an experiment in
color and emotion, physicality and aerodynamics, art
and life, thought and process, Strunk & White, dreams
and misdemeanors...

He trails off slightly mumbling, loses his place for a moment then
returns.

            Sound good, kids? Okay let's get everyone up and
            get these chairs and desks cleared out of the way.
            Walton, you and Annie give me a hand moving this
            table.

He points to an unused card table in the corner.

CUT TO:
INT. BAR – EARLY EVENING

The bartender emerges from the storeroom carrying several
bottles of liquor; he walks behind the bar and sets everything
down. He sweeps away Reily's glass and looks down the bar at
the other two guys and raises his eyebrows. The closer of the two
nods toward the men's room door. The bartender turns to look at
it and frowns.

CUT TO:

INT. BAR'S MEN'S ROOM

Reily is still looking in the mirror.

CUT TO:

EXTREME CU

A pattern of brightly colored flecks in Reily's hair.

CUT TO:

INT. CLASSROOM – MORNING

It is chaos. The children are running and throwing handfuls of goopy colors at each other, a few children are on the floor, some crying; Reily is nowhere to be seen, the classroom is a mess with colors streaked everywhere and the desks and chairs are knocked about.

CUT TO:

EXT. BAR – LATE AFTERNOON

A man walks up the sidewalk the same way that Reily came. He approaches the bar on his right; there is a car parked across the street.

CUT TO:

INT. CLASSROOM – MORNING

The laughter and screaming are just faint echoes now as four Administrators are stepping gingerly around the demolished classroom.

Walking around Reily's desk they find him lying slumped, he is smiling softly and painting his left arm with a very small brush and set of paints, the painting is an underwater scene – the sound fades to underwater sounds.

CUT TO:
INT. BAR – EARLY EVENING

The bartender is putting away some bottles. The front door bell rings, the bartender looks up.

CUT TO:

A man walks through the door and goes to sit at one of the tables. Before he gets there [FREEZE FRAME] [SLOW REVERSE] until the point where the man has just walked through the door. [FREEZE FRAME] Through the partially open door Michelle is visible walking across the street toward the bar door. [FORWARD NORMAL SPEED] The door is swinging shut, the man walks away and there is a scrape as he sits at a table.

BARTENDER
No waitress today, buddy.

CUT TO:

The man contemplates this, then gets up and crosses to the bar.

MAN
Double scotch, rocks, very little water.

BARTENDER

Four bucks.

The man slides a five dollar bill across the bar.

MAN

Keep it.

The bartender grunts his thanks

The front door bell rings, everyone stops talking and moving and looks toward the door.

CUT TO:

EXT. BAR – EVENING

A dusty, non-descript car pulls up to the spot across from the bar and parks.

CUT TO:

INT. CAR – EARLY EVENING

Michelle, a woman in her 30's with long, curly blonde hair, is behind the wheel and Tom, also in his 30's with short dark hair, is slouched in the passenger seat.

TOM

Not too long now, baby, too many people get in there it's too hard to control.

MICHELLE

Let's give it a few more minutes; too few and we don't make as much.

TOM

We're outta here after this one, right...? It's starting to get cold.

MICHELLE

Right... Of course... Where should we go, Australia?
                    (Laughs gently)

TOM

                    (Blushes and coughs reflexively)
I know, I know – we'll make it someday... It's a banana-split promise.

Tom looks out the car window at nothing and fingers the chain around his neck.

TOM (Cont.)

It wouldn't be that hard, you know, I've checked, all we have to do is focus our funds for a little while, we can get passports in Miami... We could travel around for a while, or maybe even settle down, have a place with lots of animals.

MICHELLE

Always thinking, aren't you, Mr. Lucky, and I know what a banana-split promise is... I'll hold you to it; don't think I won't.

CUT TO:

INT. HOTEL ROOM – NIGHT

Tom enters the darkened room and walks to the table they have dragged into the middle of the room. He is carrying a brown paper grocery bag. Michelle is in bed but stirs immediately when Tom enters. He sets his bag down and begins unpacking it; there are bananas, strawberries, ice cream, hot fudge in a jar, and whipped cream. Tom uncaps the fudge and puts the jar in the microwave, he sets the timer and turns it on.

                              TOM
              We've got a few minutes… So, what are you wearing?

Michelle lifts the sheet up to reveal that she is wearing only a white tank top.

CUT TO:
INT. HOTEL ROOM – NIGHT

Michelle and Tom are kissing slowly while Michelle unbuttons Tom's shirt. Unbuttoned she pulls it open and runs her fingernails down the front of his bare chest, leaving long red marks. Tom inhales sharply. The microwave shuts off and beeps.

                         MICHELLE
              I'll get a spoon.

CUT TO:
INT. CAR – EARLY EVENING

Tom and Michelle are both looking out the window for a moment. Farther down the block there are two middle-aged women walking a dog toward their car.

MICHELLE

Someone's coming. After they're gone, I say we go
for it; I want to get going, maybe make it past New
York before we stop tonight.

TOM

Mmm, Miami then?

MICHELLE

Cold drink, warm sand, and hot sex.

TOM

Now that's a plan.

*He crawls across the front seat and takes her face in his hands and
they begin to kiss.*

CUT TO:
EXT. CAR – EARLY EVENING

*The two middle-aged women walking a dog, and talking, come up
the sidewalk until they are nearly abreast of the car. They can
clearly see through the windshield Tom and Michelle locked in
embrace. The women fall silent as they pass by; they make eye
contact with each other and smile knowingly. Once past the car
they resume talking.*

DOG WALKER 1

How about those two?

DOG WALKER 2

I know, I know, I saw them... My lord, right out there
in front of God and everyone.

Oh, hey, what <u>about</u> that chocolate mousse at the
Cabots' Saturday night?

                    DOG WALKER 1
Oh... Don't even get me started. Chocolate has an
<u>effect</u> on me, you know... Stanley was sure surprised.

Both laugh; their laughter fades quickly as they walk away.

CUT TO:
INT. HOTEL ROOM – NIGHT

*Only the single bedside lamp lights the room. Tom is lying naked
on his back on the still-made bed. Michelle is straddling him. She
is holding the jar of hot fudge and a spoon; she takes a spoonful
and lets some drizzle onto Tom's chest. He gasps slightly. She
sets the jar down next to the on the bed and then leans down and
begins to lick the fudge off Tom's chest. Tom gasps again louder.*

CUT TO:
INT. CAR – EARLY EVENING

Tom and Michelle break apart from their embrace.

                    TOM
They're gone, almost to the end of the block, and it
looks like they're headed the other way.

                    MICHELLE

Let's get this over with, I know we need to eat, but I
need you and in a hurry. I think we're going to have to
find a rest area as soon as we get out of the state.

                              TOM
        Atta, baby.

They both reach beneath the seats of the car and pull out black
automatics; at the same time they check the action on the guns
and tuck them away in their waistbands, underneath their coats.
They both exit the car.

CUT TO:
EXT. CAR – EARLY EVENING

They look at each other across the top of the car for a second, and
then Tom turns and walks down the block away from the bar as
Michelle looks across the street. A man has come up the block
while they were getting out of the car and she waits while he nears
the bar. She frowns when he pulls the door open, and then shrugs
to herself and crosses the street as the man enters and the door
starts to close behind him.

CUT TO:
EXT. DOWN THE STREET – EARLY EVENING

Tom glances over his shoulder as Michelle enters the bar, and then
checks his watch. He has stopped in front of a group of posters
advertizing new movies, and he pauses to look at them and kill a
few minutes.

INT. HOTEL ROOM – NIGHT

The room is dark, candle-lit. Tom and Michelle walk together near the bed. Michelle is wearing a blue, long-sleeve men's dress shirt and Tom is wearing boxer shorts. They embrace slowly. Tom's hands slide down her back and then underneath the shirttails to her naked ass, which he squeezes. Tom kisses the back of her neck.

                    MICHELLE
                    (*Whispers*)
         Ohhhh, baby... God you make me so crazy.

CUT TO:
INT. BAR – EARLY EVENING

Michelle stands just inside the closing door. The whole room is quiet except for the TV, which rambles on in the corner. Everybody in the bar, the two near the TV, the bartender, and the man holding his drink, are staring at her. The bartender, struggling, finds his voice first.

                    BARTENDER
         Help you, Miss?

                    MICHELLE
         Ladies Room?

The bartender jerks his thumb to his right where the ladies room door is next to the men's; he never takes his eyes off her.

         Thank you. I'll take a Long Island Iced Tea for when I
         get back.

BARTENDER

Sure.

He busies himself pouring shots into a tall glass with ice.

Hey! That's the storeroom, over there, to your left.

MICHELLE

Sorryyyyyy…

*Michelle walks toward the restrooms, knowing that all eyes are on
her, she pulls open the door and disappears into the ladies room.*

CUT TO:
EXT. DOWN THE STREET – EARLY EVENING

*Tom begins humming while reading the movie posters. He checks
his watch again.*

TOM
(Singing softly)
*"Sont des mot qui vent tres bien ensemble, tres bien
ensemble."*

CUT TO:
INT. HOTEL ROOM - NIGHT

*Tom and Michelle break from their passionate embrace for a
moment.*

TOM

Wait one second, baby…

Tom walks away from Michelle. He returns carrying to gauzy scarves, one bright red and one pale green. He also has a digital camera which he turns on and aims at the bed.

CUT TO:
DIGITAL CAMERA SCREEN

Michelle stands dominating the entire frame; she is breathing evenly but looks very aroused, she looks at Tom expectantly.

CUT TO:
INT. HOTEL ROOM – NIGHT

Tom comes right up to her, pressing his body against hers, kissing her hungrily, then stops and lifts the green scarf up and slowly wraps it around her eyes and ties it in back. Michelle's breathing becomes a little irregular. Tom leaves her again; he goes behind her to rearrange the pillows on the bed, piling four of them on the middle of the white sheet.

Tom returns to Michelle and turns her so that she faces the bed. Tom slips her shirt off and drops it to the floor beside the bed.

CUT TO:
CU [SLOW MOTION]

The shirt falls to the floor near Michelle's legs and feet.

CUT TO:
INT. HOTEL ROOM – NIGHT

Michelle is lying naked with her chest on the platform of pillow, and her knees and shins on the bed. Tom enters carrying a glass of red wine. He takes a sip of the wine and knees to the floor in front of Michelle's blindfolded face. He kisses her with the wine still in his mouth and she drinks some of it while kissing him. Tom then moves around her figure where he takes her hands and ties them behind her back with the red scarf. He pauses a moment then bends down and sucks one of her fingers entirely into his mouth, Michelle gasps loudly.

CUT TO:
EXT. DOWN THE STREET – EARLY EVENING

Tom shakes off his reverie and quickly checks his watch – relieved that he's not too late; he hurries across the street and heads for the bar.

CUT TO:
DIGITAL CAMERA SCREEN

Tom takes the glass of red wine and dribbles it down her lower back and over her ass, he sets the glass back down and leans down and begins to slowly lick the wine off her skin.

CUT TO:
INT. LADIES'ROOM – EARLY EVENING

Michelle enters the Ladies Room, which is a near copy of the Men's Room. She quickly checks to make sure it empty, swinging open the doors to both stalls. Then she goes to the mirror. She looks at herself then reaches up to touch her hair.

DISSOLVE TO:
INT. HOTEL ROOM – MORNING

Tom and Michelle are lying in bed together, under the sheets. The room is till dark, but there is bright light coming from around the edges of the drawn curtains. They are both holding the digital camera and watching the small screen. They are very close together so that they can both see it. They are both making small noises and they are both squirming beneath the sheets.

                              TOM
            I love how long your hair is getting, baby, I love to
            tangle my hands into it, twist it…

He runs his open fingers through her hair and she purrs contentedly.

DISSOLVE TO:
INT. LADIES' ROOM

Michelle has both of her hands in her hair as she looks in the mirror.

CUT TO:
INT. MEN'S ROOM

Reily, with his eyes beginning to lose focus is also looking in the mirror.

CUT TO:
SPLIT SCREEN

LEFT HALF – INT. LADIES' ROOM

Michelle looking in the mirror

RIGHT HALF – INT. MEN'S ROOM

Reily looking in the mirror.

As they both turn from the mirrors there is a muffled shout from outside in the bar. They both look up.

Michelle is calm and eager; she was expecting it. Reily is curious but already distracted. He licks his lips and then opens and closes his mouth several times as if trying out the sensation. As he takes a step toward the door, Michelle takes out her gun and jacks a shell into the chamber. The sound echoes.

FADE TO BLACK

TITLE CARD:

"CAPE COD, 1977"

CUT TO:
EXT. TOP OF A SNOW-COVERED DRIVEWAY – NIGHT, SNOWING

There is a long snow-covered driveway leading to a barn and as farmhouse. The road is narrow and there are woods on the right side and a marsh on the left. The barn and farmhouse are at the end on the left past the marsh.

A car pulls up to the top of the driveway where it stops.

CUT TO:
INT. CAR – NIGHT, SNOWING

A scruffy looking, college-age guy sits behind the wheel. Jeff stubs out a cigarette in the overflowing ashtray and sighs as though he has just completed a long drive. The interior of the car is a disaster area, with empty beer cans, fast food wrappers, dirty clothes, and other junk scattered about. Jeff takes a deep breath and looks out the window. The scene is extraordinarily beautiful. He turns off his headlights and gets out of the car.

CUT TO:
EXT. TOP OF A SNOW-COVERED DRIVEWAY – NIGHT, SNOWING

Jeff stands at the top of the driveway looking down towards the barn and farmhouse. It is bright from all the snow and the driveway has not been driven on since the snow began. He climbs up onto the hood of his car and leans back against the windshield. The flakes start to stick to his hair. He reaches into his pocket of his jacket and takes out a joint and a pack of matches. He puts it to his lips and lights it. He inhales and holds it, then without releasing the smoke; he inhales again and holds it. He puts the hand holding the joint to his side and continues to hold the smoke in, his eyes bugging as his brain starves for oxygen. Finally he releases the smoke in an enormous cloud of smoke and steam.

DISSOLVES INTO SMOKE AND STEAM

CUT TO:
EXT. TOP OF A SNOW-COVERED DRIVEWAY – NIGHT, SNOWING

Jeff is asleep on the hood of his car, leaning on the windshield his head, which is covered in snow, has lolled to one side, He wakes with a start, and for a moment tries to figure out where he is. He looks down the road.

CUT TO:
EXT. BARN – NIGHT
CU

A small figure dressed sin black, wearing a black beret, comes from behind the barn and quickly crosses the road and vanishes into the wood.

CUT TO:
EXT. TOP OF A SNOW-COVERED DRIVEWAY – NIGHT, SNOWING

Jeff does a double take, almost comically exaggerated, blinks several times then looks at the joint that has gone out in his hand.

JEFF

<u>What</u> was that?

He rubs his eyes.

He gets off the hood of his car and continues to look down the road. The noticing his own footprints in the new snow, he begins walking down the road toward where the figure crossed into the woods.

Jeff continues walking and as he progresses down the road he leaves a trail of steam like a train.

From behind Jeff, where he left his car, there is the sound of a loud crash.

CUT TO:
EXT. TOP OF A SNOW-COVERED DRIVEWAY – NIGHT, SNOWING

Another car has rammed into Jeff's from behind. His car has lurched forwards and sideways, and is now half in the road and half in the marsh.

CUT TO:
INT. FARMHOUSE KITCHEN – MORNING

In the brightly-lit kitchen a woman in her 50's, Lily, is dialing a telephone. A small girl about 8 or 9, Shelley, is clearing breakfast dishes and putting them into the dishwasher.

LILY
Hello, Meredith? It's Lily. I don't know what happened; Charles called a cab first thing and Jeffie's still asleep; both cars are wrecked, and Mr. Mullen, you know Bobby Mullen's father? He's been doing my plowing for years, wonderful man, very distinguished widower, anyway he said Jeff's car is half in the marsh and that Charles' may be totaled.

Lily listens for a moment and looks over at Shelley.

Yes, she's still here.

I don't know.

I <u>don't</u> know.

Well, the mother has the Memorial Drive condo, for
her and her pottery types, and you know how Charles
had been so <u>wrapped</u> up in this deal.

She's still on her winter vacation, but she needs to go
somewhere soon.

*She looks over to where Shelley is finishing the dishes and closing
the dishwater.*

Meredith, I have to go.

Uh, huh.

She hangs up the phone on the wall and turns back to Shelley.

Thank you, Shelley, now I'd like you to go get the mail
for me, please. I wouldn't be able to turn my car
around.

SHELLEY
Yes, Grandma.

*Lily frowns slightly at hearing this, but then turns and walks out of
the kitchen.*

Shelley exits the kitchen from a different door.

CUT TO:
INT. INSIDE FARMHOUSE BACK DOOR

Shelley sits on the floor near the door, struggling into winter boots; her coats, hat and mittens are piled next to her. Finally she stands and pulls on her coat. She reaches for the handle on the big door.

CUT TO:
INT. JEFF'S BEDROOOM – MORNING

Jeff lies sleeping under rumpled quilts. The already messy room is dark but brightening. There is a tattered poster depicting Superman on the wall above the bed. Jeff begins to stir, stretching his arms slowly.

CUT TO:
INT. FARMHOUSE KITCHEN – MORNING

Jeff shuffles into the kitchen whistling tunelessly with a sleepy and empty look on his face. He is barefoot, wearing boxer shorts, a t-shirt and an old robe that drapes open. He takes cereal from the kitchen cupboard and pours some into a large bowl, then takes milk from the refrigerator and adds that, with a spoon he sits at the table and begins to eat, the cereal crunching noisily.

Lily enters through the same door she had earlier exited.

> JEFF
> (Mumbles)
Morning, Mom.

> LILY

Jeffrey, what in God's name happened to your cars?
Charles left this morning before he could tell me. How
did they get wrecked like that? You know I can't get
out, don't you? You do realize the snowplow man
can't get in? He's the one who called me this morning
at 6 AM, asking what he should do. What if there were
an emergency? Jeff, are you listening? What are we
going to do about this, and exactly what happened to
your cars?

                        JEFF
        My car?

Jeff takes more than half a beat to focus.

CUT TO:
EXT. THE TOP OF THE SNOW-COVERED DRIVEWAY – NIGHT

*Jeff sitting on the hood of his car peers through the snow, which is
increasing in his recollection. The figure, which at this distance
could be anything, moves like a quick shadow.*

CUT TO:
INT. FARMHOUSE KITCHEN – MORNING

Jeff snaps to with a start.

                        JEFF
        Be right back.

*He jumps from the table and runs out of the room, as he runs his
robe flaps behind him like a cape.*

LILY

Jeffie, where are you going? Jeffie? Jeffery!

She is speaking to an empty room.

CUT TO:
INT. FARMHOUSE LIVING ROOM – MORNING

Jeff runs through the living room, the furniture rattles at his all-out abandon, he exits the far side at top speed.

CUT TO:
EXT. FARMHOUSE – MORNING

Jeff burst out the side door and runs, barefoot through the snow, towards the spot in the driveway where the figure had crossed the road. He obviously is looking for foot prints, but it has snowed all night, and the only prints are Charles', heading up the driveway to the road. He stands around for a while looking on both sides of the road, until he feet start getting cold and he has to hop.

Lily sticks her head out of the door and sees Jeff hopping around barefoot in the snow.

LILY

(*Yells almost hysterically*)
Are you insane! Get back in the house this instant. I will have you institutionalized!

Jeff looks at her absently, then still hopping heads back to the door.

CUT TO:

INT. FARMHOUSE KITCHEN – MORNING

Jeff sits back down at the table and while chewing his cereal appears to be deep in thought.

Lily is staring at him as though he were a very weird insect.

> LILY
>
> Dinner is at 7PM tonight, Jeff, please, be on time.

Jeff murmurs something vague and vacant through a mouthful of cereal.

CUT TO:

INT. BUSINESS OFFICE – MORNING

Charles is sitting at the desk in his office; he is on the phone while at the same time sorting through various piles of paper on his desk. He appears very stressed.

> CHARLES
>
> It's 433 Gray Gables Road, all the way at the end of Shore Road.

His intercom sounds.

> INTERCOM MONICA
>
> Charles your meeting with the partners is in 15 minutes.

> CHARLES

(*Sounding anxious*)
Thank you, Monica; I'm almost ready.

INTERCOM MONICA

Are you all right Charles? Would you like some water
or coffee?

TOW TRUCK DRIVER ON PHONE
(*Sarcastically*)
Yeah, Charles, are you a'right, buddy?

Charles puts his hand to his head.

CHARLES

Please, please go and get my car, you have the
address, it's a dark green Cadillac, it rear-ended an
old Galaxy 500.

TOW TRUCK DRIVER ON PHONE

It did, huh? Whatta 'bout the Ford, you want that
towed too?

Charles straightens up firmly.

CHARLES

No, that's my brother's vehicle; I am certain he will
make his own arrangements.

TOW TRUCK DRIVER ON PHONE

A'right buddy, to your mechanic, right? 150 bucks,
your mechanic will bill you.

He hangs up abruptly leaving Charles holding the receiver. His
intercom sounds again.

                    INTERCOM MONICA
          Charles, 10 minutes until your meeting and it's up on
          17...

                        CHARLES
          Right, right, just gathering my papers.

                    INTERCOM MONICA
          Your wife called while you were talking to the garage,
          she says she will be in Vermont through New Years;
          she left an address, a Post Office box... But there's
          also a phone number.

                        CHARLES
                    (Muffled, mumbled)
          Thank you, Monica.

INT. FARMHOUSE STORAGE ROOM – AFTERNOON

A large dark room filled with overcoats, foul weather gear,
numerous dressers, cupboards, and chests containing decades'
worth of hunting, fishing, camping, athletic and aquatic pursuits.

Jeff is rummaging through various drawers and cupboards,
looking for and selecting various camping and hunting artifacts.
He piles them on the floor.

                        LILY

(*Muffled and faint*)
Jeff! Jeffieeeeeee! Where are you?

CUT TO:

INT. FARMHOUSE FRONT HALL – AFTERNOON

Lily is looking up the stairs.

                         LILY

             Jeff? Shelley? Where is everyone?

CUT TO:

INT. FARMHOUSE BATHROOM – LATE AFTERNOON

Jeff stands in front of the mirror above the sink. He is dressed in a
black sweater and black watch cap; he is holding a lit match to a
wine cork. It smokes furiously and he stubs it out against the sink.
Taking the burnt cork he begins drawing it across his face,
smudging black in long strokes.

CUT TO:

INT. FARMHOUSE KITCHEN – LATE AFTERNOON

Lily is speaking into the handset of a wall-mounted phone with an
extremely long cord. She is tending a few pots on the stove.

                         LILY

             You will be home early for dinner, won't you Charles?
             Did you rent a car? What about your Cadillac, can it
             be fixed?

She moves to the oven which she opens – there is a large beef roast inside, surrounded by potatoes. She closes the door.

Well make sure to get a head start on the Friday traffic, you know even in winter in can be awful near the bridge.

CUT TO:
INT. OFFICE – ALMOST SUNSET

Charles hangs up the phone. He looks exhausted, drained, and a little bit rumpled. There are two partly-filled boxes on his desk, they contain personal items and his desk is almost empty besides the boxes. He opens a drawer and pulls out a framed photo of himself and a woman. He looks at for a second before dumping it into one of the boxes.

INTERCOM MONICA
Charles, a gentleman has just dropped off the keys to your rental car. He says it is a dark blue Chrysler, parked right across the street from the building.

CHARLES
(In monotone)
Thank you, Monica, I'm almost finished here, I'll pick them up on my way out.

INTERCOM MONICA
I'm sorry Charles… Truly I am.

CHARLES
(Quietly)

Yes.

INTERCOM MONICA

Will you be all right? Is there anything I can for you?
Are you going back to your mother's tonight?

*Charles doesn't answer but turns and looks out the window at the
setting sun.*

CUT TO:
INT. FARMHOUSE DINING ROOM – SUNSET

*Shelley is setting four places at the table. The table already is
beautiful with a brilliant white tablecloth and flowers in the center
and candles at either end. She puts down the plates firs, and then
goes to a sideboard for silverware, carefully setting two forks, a
spoon and a knife at each place. She leaves the dining room.*

Through a window, Jeff can be seen exiting a side door.

CUT TO:
EXT. FARMHOUSE – SUNSET

*Jeff, wearing or carrying all his gear, leaves the house and crosses
the road into the woods.*

CUT TO:
EXT. WOODS – SUNSET

*After some searching Jeff finds a likely tree and begins to haul his
gear up to a fork about six feet off the ground. He ties everything
down and creates a shelf to sit on. With everything ready, he*

settles onto his perch and leans back against the trunk. He pulls out a thermos and pours some steaming coffee into the cup.

CUT TO:
EXT. OFFICE BUILDING – SUNDOWN

Charles is loading his boxes into the trunk of the Chrysler. He closes the trunk firmly and pauses for a long moment before turning on his heel and heading down the street toward a well-lit tavern.

CUT TO:
INT. TAVERN – EVENING

Charles sits down at a fairly crowded bar; he nods at the bartender in silent recognition. The bartender does the same and efficiently sets a neat glass of scotch in front of Charles.

CUT TO:
INT. FARMHOUSE LIVING ROOM – EVENING
[MUSIC]

Lily is sitting in a formal living room listening to classical music. She is dressed very nicely, wearing an elegant but conservative evening dress. There is sadness fighting with irritation on her face.

Shelley enters the room, walking very carefully so as not to spill the cocktail glass she is carrying. She crosses the room to Lily and sets the glass on a coaster next to her.

CUT TO:

INT. FARMHOUSE LIVING ROOM – EVENING

*The music is coming to an end, Lily swirls the remainder of her ice
and drink, and takes a last sip.*

*Shelley is sitting alone on a large couch with legs and Mary Janes
dangling. She also sips her cocktail.*

CUT TO:
EXT. WOODS – NIGHT

*Jeff sits on his perch in the tree: finishing his coffee, he screws the
cap back on the thermos. Digging into the pocket of his black
anorak he extracts a joint and a pack of matches, He puts the joint
to his lips and lights it, inhaling deeply and several times. He sits
absolutely still for a minute, his eyes bugging, his face reddening
around the black streaks of burnt cork. When he releases the
lungful of smoke, combined with steam in the cold night, it billows
voluminously.*

CUT TO:
EXT. THE SKY - DAYTIME
[SPECIAL EFFECTS]

*Jeff is dressed like Superman flying. He emerges from the clouds
into the blue sky and as he flies he focuses his super vision to
spot a leprechaun frolicking in a large field filled with marijuana
plants. He smiles serenely and alters his course to aim for the
field.*

CUT TO:
INT. TAVERN – EVENING

Charles sits at the crowded bar by himself. There is an attractive woman next to him, and he offers her a wan half-smile, which she ignores and turns to speak to the woman on her other side.

Charles catches the eye of the bartender and touches the rim of his empty glass.

CUT TO:
INT. FARMHOUSE DINING ROOM – EVENING

Lily enters the dining room; at the table the candles are lit. Shelley is standing behind the chair that is pulled out.

Lily crosses to the chair and sits down. Shelley helps her scoot her chair in.

LILY

> Thank you, Shelley. We won't wait. Would you please carve the roast?

An interested looks crosses Shelley's face.

Lily serves herself some vegetables from a dish.

Shelley approaches the roast and picks up the huge knife and fork.

CUT TO:
EXT. WOODS

Jeff is still up in his tree perch and is now sleeping peacefully.

CUT TO:

INT. FARMHOUSE DINING ROOM

Lily pours herself a glass of red wine. There is a glass of milk in a heavy glass at Shelley's place to her left.

Shelley is butchering the meat with great concentration.

The other two place settings are still empty.

CUT TO:

EXT. TAVERN – NIGHT

Charles leaves the tavern; he walks a little unsteadily to his rental car. He drops the keys once and has to stoop to retrieve them before unlocking the unfamiliar car.

CUT TO:

INT CAR (DRIVING) – NIGHT

Charles is on the highway driving into the black. His face is slowly crumbling with stress, weariness, sadness, and futility.

CUT TO:

INT. FARMHOUSE DINING ROOM – EVENING

Lily and Shelley are sitting at the table eating – the silverware tinkles against the china.

Lily pours herself some more wine.

LILY

Pour yourself some more milk, Shelley, I'd like to
make a toast.

*Shelley stands and pours more milk into her glass from a silver
pitcher; she sits back down. Lily lifts her glass.*

LILY
(*In a softer tone*)
Lift your glass, dear.

Shelley picks up her glass and holds it up.

A toast: To all the loathsome, despicable, unreliable
and thoughtless men out there... That is to say, to all
of them... And to you and me, Shelley, it has been a
lovely dinner, thank you.

CUT TO:

*Lily sits at the table, finishing her wine. Shelley is making trips
back and forth from the table to the kitchen, clearing dishes.*

CUT TO:

*The table cleared, Shelley enters the room and walks up to Lily's
place. She sets a small, poorly wrapped gift on the table in front of
Lily.*

SHELLEY
Happy Birthday, Grandma.

Lily says nothing, just stares at the small package.

Shelley turns and quickly leaves the room.

CUT TO:
EXT. FARMHOUSE BACK DOOR – NIGHT

Shelley exits the farmhouse by the back door, which is a fairly dark area. She is dressed in black pants and a black sweater. Her blonde curls are stuffed up into a black beret. She is carrying a small paper bag. She quickly walks behind the barn and around, headed for the crossing that Jeff is staking out. By circling the barn, she avoids the well-lit parking area. She moves quickly until she reaches the road where she pauses before running across and disappearing into the woods.

CUT TO:
INT. FARMHOUSE LILY'S BEDROOM – NIGHT

Lily slowly moves about her bedroom as she makes her final preparations for bed. She is wearing a full-length, flannel nightgown, and her bedside lamp is on and her sheets turned down. She closes the door to her room and sits on the edge of the bed for a moment, as if to take off her slippers but she doesn't. The package that Shelley gave her is sitting on her bedside table and she stares at it.

CUT TO:
EXT. EMPTY HIGHWAY, WOODS ON BOTH SIDES – NIGHT

Charles races down the highway in his rental car.

CUT TO:

INT. CAR (DRIVING) NIGHT

Charles' hands grip the wheel in a variety of ways and he seems near to tears.

CUT TO:
INT. FARMHOUSE LILY'S BEDROOM – NIGHT

Lily slides her legs under the sheets and blankets and pulls them up around her. On her bedside table is a hardcover book about the history of Cape Cod; she picks it up for a moment. She sets it back down and picks up Shelley's present. She turns it over several times in her hands.

CUT TO:
EXT. WOODS – NIGHT

Jeff is still asleep in the tree, smiling at his dreams. He shifts himself in his sleep and lets out a long steamy sigh.

DISSOLVE TO:
EXT. WOODS – NIGHT

Jeff is still smiling in his sleep and doesn't hear the small, crunchy footsteps. Shelley appears beneath Jeff's perch and walks by, neither aware of the other. Shelley walks deeper into the woods where she stops in a moon-lit opening. Just at the edge is a small dugout den. Inside are two small fox kits snuggled behind a dark wool blanket. Shelley unpacks some leftover roast beef from her bag and begins feeding it to the foxes.

Jeff is still sleeping in the tree.

The long driveway is quiet and still blanketed in snow.

Jeff's car is at the top of the road still partially blocking the
driveway.

Charles slams his rental car into the back of Jeff's, again, the snow
on it explodes upwards in slow motion like fireworks.

FADE TO BLACK

CUT TO:
INT. HOTEL ROOM – MIDNIGHT

Michelle and Tom are in bed, lying together in candlelight. They
are both breathing slightly heavily and are damp with perspiration
where the sheet isn't sticking to their bodies, outlining them.
Tom's arm is around her and her head lies on his chest. Her hand
absently strokes his belly.

                    TOM
        I can't remember what life was like before we met…

Michelle lifts her head and kisses Tom's chest.

        … Really, it's like everything before is gone, I know it
        sounds crazy…

                    MICHELLE
        Mmm, baby….

She gently kisses the round, puckered scar, high on his shoulder.

But we've only been together a few months.

                    TOM
Pretty nice months, though.

                  MICHELLE
Oh, baby,

She slowly, deliberately bites his nipple. Tom inhales sharply.

You know it's the best...

She rolls over until she is lying face down on his chest.

... You drive me absolutely wild – I can't ever let you
go.

                    TOM
Forever's a long time, how about if we try a couple
hundred years and see how it goes?

                  MICHELLE
I think I can clear my schedule.

Tom twists his fingers through Michelle's hair.

                    TOM
I love you, baby.

                  MICHELLE
Me, too.

TOM
(*Grinning in the dark*)
I know, baby, and you are just the cutest.

MICHELLE
Did anyone ever tell you that you are too smart for
your own good?

FADE TO BLACK

CUT TO:
INT. HOTEL ROOM – EARLY MORNING

*Soft light is seeping around the heavy curtains. Michelle is
dressed in sweatpants and a sweater. She quietly exits the room.
Tom continues to sleep.*

CUT TO:
Tom sleeping.

CUT TO:
Tom sleeping.

*The magnetic lock on the hotel room door clicks and then opens.
Michelle enters, moving quietly, looking to see if Tom is still
asleep. She is carrying a pastry bag and two cups of take-out
coffee.*

*Tom is just barely starting to wake up. Michelle quickly strips off
her sweatpants and sweater; she is naked beneath. She slips back
under the sheets and blanket and snuggles up to Tom.*

MICHELLE
(*Softly purring*)
Morning, Sunshine.

TOM
(*Groggily*)
Morning, baby.

CUT TO:
INTO. HOTEL ROOM – EARLY MORNING

Tom and Michelle are having sex beneath the sheet. They climax together, moaning deeply, gasping, kissing and biting each other's necks as they spasm together.

CUT TO:
INT. HOTEL ROOM – EARLY EVENING

Tom is sitting in a pair of boxer shorts on the desk chair. He is spinning around, back and forth, changing directions.

The toilet flushes and Michelle comes out of the bathroom.

MICHELLE
How about some breakfast?

Tom looks at the coffee and pastry that he hadn't noticed before.

TOM
Mmm, coffee, sure, I'm starving.

MICHELLE

I got some scones, cranberry and blueberry.

TOM

Never had one, of any kind.

Michelle hands Tom one of the cups of coffee and then taking one of the scone, she climbs into Tom's lap, straddling him. She slowly and carefully breaks off a piece of scone and puts it in Tom's mouth. As he chews, his face betrays his enjoyment. Michelle eats a piece herself. Then as she breaks off another piece and even more slowly puts it into his mouth, Tom's expression changes as Michelle starts to slowly move her hips back and forth.

TOM

I could learn to love breakfast…

FADE TO BLACK

TITLE CARD:

"BREAKFAST AT TIFFANY'S, 1985"

CUT TO:

EXT. SUBURBAN NEIGHBORHOOD – MORNING

[VERY HIGH CONTRAST, VERY BRIGHT]

Three gang members in leather jackets ride their motorcycles through a quiet, sundrenched suburban street. One, clearly the leader (a younger Tom), motions with his head at a 7-11 on the corner. The other two nod and pull into the parking lot and come to a stop. They dismount and watch him continue down the street almost to the end of the block where he too stops. They look at each other and shrug; they go into the 7-11.

CUT TO:
EXT. 7-11 – MORNING

The two emerge from the store carrying Yoo-Hoos and Hostess cupcakes. They walk back to their bikes and look down the street to where Tommy is parked. He is sitting back on his bike doing nothing.

They rip open their purchases and start eating them hungrily.

> FIRST
> *(Squinting down the street)*
> What's Tommy doin'?

> SECOND
> Still just sittin' there. Man, I hate this shit, someone could smoke him so easy.

He stuffs the last of his cupcake in his mouth and then pulls a pint bottle of vodka from his leather jacket and pours it into his half-empty Yoo-Hoo bottle.

> What should we do?

He shakes the bottle vigorously.

> FIRST
> He said wait; we wait.

The Second shrugs and takes a long drink from his spiked Yoo-Hoo.

CUT TO:
EXT. TIFFANY'S HOUSE – MORNING

Tommy sits on his bike across the street from Tiffany's house; he sits patiently as if awaiting nothing. His leather jacket is partially open and the butt of a black automatic in a shoulder holster is visible beneath it against a white t-shirt.

Nearby a neighbor in shorts, black socks and sandals, his white legs gleaming, works on his shrubs with electric clippers. Two elderly ladies with their hair in curlers chat on the front step of a house just past. No one seems to notice Tommy or his motorcycle.

INT. TIFFANY'S BEDROOM – MORNING

Gauzy curtains are letting a diffused light. A young guy, Tiffany's cousin, lies in a rumpled bed. Tiffany is just leaving the bedroom, she is naked.

TIFFANY
>(*Over her shoulder, halfway out the door*)
>How about some breakfast? I could use a morning pick-me-up.

[FREEZE FRAME]

Tiffany is halfway through the door, looking back over her shoulder.

COUSIN – VOICE OVER

That's Tiffany... I've been in love with her since we
were babies.

CUT TO:
INT. NURSERY [FUZZY] – HARSH DAYLIGHT

*Two 1960's moms, who look similar to each other and are wearing
the same style clothes, stare down at two babies in a crib wriggling
around together.*

COUSIN – VOICE OVER

That's us, and our Moms. It took me over twenty
years to get her into bed again. But it was worth the
wait.

CUT TO:
INT. TIFFANY'S BEDROOM – MORNING

COUSIN

Sure, Tiff, sounds great.

He rolls onto his back and stretches.
[FREEZE FRAME]

The cousin is caught in mid-stretch, his face contorted happily.

COUSIN – VOICE OVER

And that's me. Tiffany's cousin; her first cousin
actually. Our mothers are sisters. We grew up
together for a while – same nursery school and

kindergarten. Then we went to separate boarding
schools and I only saw her on vacations.

CUT TO:
EXT. TIFFANY'S HOUSE – MORNING

The neighbor works meticulously on his shrubs; carefully making
sure the entire side that faces the street is flat. His back is to
Tommy.

CUT TO:
INT. TIFFANY'S BEDROOM – MORNING

The cousin gets out of bed and slides on a pair of white briefs. He
stretches again, to his toes, and then starts to wander around
Tiffany's bedroom, looking at her stuff, snooping a little.

COUSIN – VOICE OVER

Who knows what law is where, but this isn't
Tennessee and I'm pretty sure sleeping with your first
cousin is some kind of no-no here; whether it's a
felony, taboo, or just frowned upon, I had a feeling the
best we could hope for was frowns. I really didn't
care. This was so much better that the time we went
skinny dipping that summer we were 16.

CUT TO:
EXT. END OF A DOCK – LATE NIGHT

Two teenagers are in the black water together. Their clothes are
piled at the end of the dock as well as several empty beer cans.

The two are laughing and shivering in the chilly water and moonlight.

TIFFANY

Okay, try it again... *Un, deux, trois, quatre...*

COUSIN

Un, deux, trois, quatre...

Tiffany laughs some more.

TIFFANY

At this rate we'll drown before you can count to ten in French.

CUT TO:
INT. TIFFANY'S BEDROOM – MORNING

The cousin catches sight of Tommy through a gap in the curtains and is immediately curious. He moves to the window and crouches down in front of it.

CUT TO:
EXT. 7-11 – MORNING

The two gang members stand watching down the block, but less and less scrupulously. The First absentmindedly pulls out a pocketknife and picks at his fingernails.

SECOND

Do you think this shit is about that chick again? He's lying on her house down there, ain't he? Shit, I

thought that was over, he could have been wasted last
time.

                    FIRST
          I know, bro, I was there too, that pretty-boy fucker
          shot me in the neck.

He pulls the collar of his jacket away to display freshly healed scar.

                    SECOND
          Dude, I took two in the fuckin' gut from those same
          cocksuckers last year!

*Now he lifts his t-shirt to expose a white belly webbed with pink
scars.*

                    FIRST
          So what, you pussy, how 'bout when that little zip
          tried to carve me up...

He turns and begins lifting the back of his jacket and shirt.

CUT TO:
EXT. TIFFANY'S HOUSE – MORNING

*The neighbor keeps working on his shrubs, turning a sharp corner
onto the first short side. The two elderly ladies chat some more,
chuckle together, and then enter their houses. The neighbor
pauses for a moment, removes his hat and wipes his brow. He still
does not notice Tommy.*

CUT TO:

INT. TIFFANY'S BEFROOM – MORNING

The cousin continues to watch out the window, keeping himself low, although Tommy is not looking at the second floor at all. He is kneeling on the floor with his hands on the windowsill.

CUT TO:
EXT. TIFFANY'S HOUSE – MORNING

The neighbor makes the turn around his hedge and starts clipping the long side now facing the street.

CUT TO:
EXT. 7-11 – MORNING

Both gang members have their shirts and jackets up, exposing their scarred torsos; their muffled claims of past injury come from inside their leather jackets.

[SLOW MOTION]

Behind them, a Camaro with tinted windows creeps by and passes them without their noticing.

CUT TO:
INT. DINGY BEDROOM – EARLIER THAT MORNING
[SILENT & SLOW MOTION]

A young man with slicked-back hair stands facing a mirror on the wall. He pulls on a pristine white linen shirt and meticulously tucks it into his pants. Satisfied he spins on his heel and strides out of the room.

CUT TO:

INT. LIVING ROOM – MORNING

[SILENT & SLOW MOTION]

The young man enters the living room and nods at the heavily tattooed enforcer sitting on the couch. The enforcer nods in response and knocks back a shot of a harsh-looking yellow liquid with only a trace of a grimace.

CUT TO:

EXT. ALLEY WAY – MORNING

[SILENT & SLOW MOTION]

The young man and the enforcer emerge from a junk-strewn backyard and get into a tricked-out Camaro; the young man drives.

The car pulls forward.

CUT TO:

EXT. CITY STREETS – MORNING

[SILENT & SLOW MOTION]

The Camaro passes under a highway overpass, heading out of the inner city and into the suburbs.

CUT TO:

INT. CAMARO – MORNING

[SILENT & SLOW MOTION]

The enforcer checks his shotgun. Through the window there is a 7-11 a few blocks ahead.

CUT TO:
EXT. TIFFANY'S HOUSE – MORNING
[SILENT & SLOW MOTION]

The Camaro slides to a stop and the passenger leaps out with the shotgun. Tommy shoots him, three shots dropping him immediately. The young guy gets out on the far side of the car; Tommy's gun jams. The young guy fires across the top of the car with a small, pearl-handled automatic, hitting Tommy in the shoulder. Tommy goes down from his bike, and out of the shooter's view. The shooter walks around the front of the Camaro and toward Tommy.

CUT TO:
[SILENT & SLOW MOTION]

Tiffany bursts from her house, nude, screaming.

CUT TO:

The young guy without even looking fires at Tiffany and keeps walking toward Tommy. Then he is over him and he pauses, adjusting his cuffs, then aims carefully at Tommy who is reaching out, trying to reach his own gun, lying well away.

CUT TO:

The young guy's back is riddled with shots, red spots appearing on his white shirt as his body dances involuntarily.

The First and Second rush up having sprinted down the block, too late, they continue firing with heavy automatics in each hand until the body drops to the street.

The First runs and scoops up Tommy while the Second puts several superfluous blasts into the passenger of the Camaro. The First puts Tommy in the Camaro and runs to the driver's side. The Second jumps on Tommy's bike and shoots forward. The Camaro follows.

[WIDE ANGLE]

The neighborhood is quiet and still again. There are two bodies in the street; the neighbor's legs are sticking out of the hedge where he must have dove during the commotion; Tiffany is lying naked at the bottom of her front steps; the cousin is looking out the window, stunned.

FADE TO BLACK

DISSOLVE TO:
INT. FANCY RESTAURANT - EVENING

It is a crowded, elegant dining room. Tom and Michelle are seated at an intimate table for two. They are dressed in nice clothes, a suit and tie for Tom, and a sexy black dress and stockings for Michelle. They are finishing their dinner and sipping their wine; they talk quietly, touching hands every once in a while.

The waiter clears their places.

CUT TO:

The waiter delivers chocolate mousse and champagne. They share one dish and clink their glasses more than once.

Under the table, Michelle slips her high-heeled pump off and runs her stockinged foot up the inside of Tom's leg.

CUT TO:
INT. FANCY RESTAURANT, DANCE FLOOR - EVENING

Tom and Michelle are dancing together among several much older couples. They are moving slowly together, pressed tight, completely in their own universe.

CUT TO:
INT. HOTEL ROOM – LATER SAME EVENING

Tom and Michelle enter the room, holding each other, slightly drunk, kissing, laughing and crashing through the door. Once in and the door swings shut, they part lingeringly. Michelle throws the deadbolt and puts on the chain; Tom empties the pockets of his jacket and walks to the bar. He pours some red wine into a low glass tumbler. He takes a long sip and hands the glass to Michelle. They both close their eyes and continue to kiss for a long moment, embracing tenderly. They part slowly and Tom slips off his jacket, throwing it over a chair. They never take their eyes off each other. Michelle pulls unzips her dress and lets it fall to the floor. She is wearing black stockings held up by a garter belt, and black panties and bra. She steps out of her fallen dress and walks to their luggage. She reaches into a travel bag and pulls out a pair of handcuffs; she turns and holds them dangling in front of Tom, smiling slightly.

                              TOM
          Ohh, baby… You always know just what to say…

He turns and puts his hands together behind his back.

CUT TO:
INT. BAR - EVENING
CU – MEN'S ROOM DOOR

The door opens and Reily slowly moves through it. He takes a
step and then stops; his face looks puzzled.

CUT TO:
INT. BAR – DUSK

Reily stands outside the men's room door. The bartender is
standing tensely behind the bar, looking like he wants to do
something, anything. The two guys who had been watching the TV
are lying face down on the floor as is the man from the tables.
Tom is standing over him, holding a gun, beckoning for the man's
wallet.

                              TOM
          Let's go; let's go… Quickly, please; your watch too.

The man, still lying on the floor, slides his watch off his wrist and
lifts it up. Tom is not looking at him but slowly covering the whole
room with his gun, eyeing the bartender carefully.

CUT TO:

CU – Reily's head, his eyes are wet and move slowly, uncomprehending.

                    REILY
          Arnold? What on earth is go-

All of a sudden Reily's head is snapped back and the barrel of a gun is stuck into the soft skin under his jaw.

CUT TO:
INT. BAR – EVENING

Tom immediately looks at them and his gun goes back and forth between the bartender and Reily, whose hair is being held by Michelle, her gun still pressed under his jaw.

                    TOM
          Nobody move…

He moves his gun again from Reily to the bartender.

          Everything okay, baby?

Michelle nods although Reily is already starting to be a problem. He cannot stop his body from weaving and his right knee is buckling slightly.

                    MICHELLE
                    (Hisses)
          Stand up!

CUT TO:

PERSPECTIVE OF MAN ON THE FLOOR

Looking straight across the floor, to one side are Tom's feet, and a little further is the man's whiskey glass lying empty on its side.

CUT TO:
INT. BAR – EVENING

TOM

Okay, deep breath everyone, let's get back to it.

He slowly steps away from the man on the floor; as he goes to set his foot down his heel comes down on the edge of the glass causing it to roll slightly. Tom momentarily has to catch his balance.

The bartender seizes his chance and snatches the shotgun from beneath the bar.
[SLOW MOTION]

He raise the gun to his shoulder, points it across the bar, and fires.

[SHOT ECHOES]
FADE TO BLACK

VOICE OVER

Shelley?

[ECHO FADES]

Shel? Are you awake? It's almost 7, the twins will be up soon.

CUT TO:

INT. BEDROOM – MORNING

CU – Shelley opens her eyes.
[FAINT GUNSHOT ECHO FADES TO NOTHING]

CUT TO:

INT. BEDROOM – MORNING

The sound of the radio comes from an open bathroom door.
Shelley lies in bed not moving. Mike stands in front of the mirror,
trying to knot his tie.

> MIKE
>
> Are you up? How late were you reading last night?
> I've got to get moving, just heard some noise from the
> twins' room, I'd expect an invasion soon.

Mike undoes his tie and starts over.

> What are you doing today?

CUT TO:

Shelley lying in bed.

CUT TO:

INT. BOOKSTORE – THE DAY BEFORE

Shelley is standing near the cash register, frozen in place as she
looks at a flyer posted near the cash register.

CUT TO:

CU - The *flyer announces the appearance of the author, V. Reily,
signing copies of his novel, "Collision". There is a small picture of
him.*

CUT TO:

CASHIER
With tax that's going to be $28.04.

*Shelley continues to look at the flyer, but slides her Visa card
across the counter.*

CUT TO:

EXTREME CU – *The picture of Reily from the flyer. It is grainy and
black and white but obviously him.*

CUT TO:
INT. BEDROOM – MORNING

*Shelley is still lying in bed; on the table next to her bed there is a
copy of the book "Collision" sitting beneath the lamp next to a
bottle of nighttime lotion.*

SHELLEY
I need to go back to the bookstore.

She thinks for a moment.

Mike, do you think your mother could pick up the
twins from preschool? I may be late.

*Mike doesn't seem to hear though; having knotted his tie
imperfectly he crosses the room and opens the bedroom door to
the hallway. At that moment two three-year old girls in nightgowns
burst through the doorway laughing.*

TWINS
(Together)
Mommy, mommy, mommy, mommy, mommy...

They jump on the bed and start trying to tickle their mother.

CUT TO:

Mike disappears into the hallway.

CUT TO:

*Shelley puts her head under her pillow causing the two girls to
squeal in delight as they too try to get their heads under the pillow
that Shelley has clamped over her head.*

CUT TO:
INT. BEDROOM – MORNING

*Shelley sits at her dressing table looking in the mirror. She is
wearing black pants and a black bra. Behind her the twins are
jumping on the bed.*

CUT TO:

INT. REILY'S APARTMENT LIVING ROOM – NIGHT

Reily sits at a personal computer slowly typing; there is a large bandage above a bruised and puffy eye.

CUT TO:
EXT. PRESCHOOL – MORNING
[MUSIC]

Shelley's car pulls up in front of the preschool. She gets out of the car; she is wearing tight black pants, a black turtleneck and a fashionable leather jacket. She opens the back door of her car and the twins get out. She shepherds them in the front door amongst other parents doing the same. After a minute she reappears alone and gets back in her car.

CUT TO:
BEDROOM – EARLIER

Shelley sits at her dressing table, in her mirror the twins are visible jumping on the bed, laughing and swinging pillows at each other.

Shelley looks at herself in the mirror, ignoring the twins. She reaches for a small jewelry box and opens an even smaller drawer. From inside she pulls out a chain with the key on the end. The steel is dull and brown; she holds it for a moment before lifting it over her head.

CUT TO:
EXTREME CU
[SLOW MOTION]

Shelley's throat and chest. The key at the end of the chain slides down Shelley's throat and chest and slides out of sight in her décolletage and bra.

CUT TO:
EXT. BOOKSTORE – MORNING

Shelley parks next to one of a few cars in the parking lot; she doesn't get out. She reaches between her legs and beneath the car seat.

CUT TO:
INT. BOOKSTORE – MIDMORNING

Reily sits at a table with a small stack of his books next to him. There are a couple of customers and bookstore employees milling about, chatting, sipping wine, and nearly ignoring Reily. Reily sits alone looking straight out the front window at the parking lot.

He takes a sip of white wine from a plastic cup.

CUT TO:
CU – Reily's face is pulled back so he's almost looking up; the gun is still pressed hard into his jaw. He tries to open his mouth.

CUT TO:
INT. BAR – EVENING
                              REILY
                      (A croaky whisper)
            Please, Miss…

Michelle twists the gun into him tighter.

The bartender reaches below the bar and snatches the shotgun; he levels it and fires across the bar at Tom. Tom goes down in a bloody heap.

> MICHELLE
> (Screaming)

No...

Michelle immediately swings her gun and fires at the bartender four times rapidly, the mirror and many bottles behind him explode. The bartender ducks down behind the bar, apparently un-hit.

Michelle jams the gun back into Reily's neck and pivots him so that his body is between her and the bar. She starts to sideways walk him across the room to where Tom went down. Her eyes are still wild, but tears are beginning to well up in them. When she and Reily reach the spot where Tom lays, Michelle fires twice more over the bar above the ducking bartender. She looks down at Tom, but there is no hope, his chest has a gaping bloody hole in it. She fires at the same spot again and then, in one quick motion, ducks down and pulls the chain from over Tom's head. Her hand comes up bloody, the chain dangling.

CUT TO:

CU – Michelle's hand with the chain dangling. Her fingers and the chain are covered in blood.
[SLOW MOTION]

She spins the chain with the key at the end around. Droplets of blood fly away. Her fingers come out and the chain wraps around her hand until the key hits her palm. Her hand closes.

CUT TO:

EXT. BAR – NIGHT

Michelle backs out the door to the bar dragging Reily by his hair after her. Before they let the door close she takes two more shots at the ducking bartender, more out of frustration and anger that any real hope of hitting him. She tries to fire again but her gun clicks twice on the empty chamber. The bar door closes and they are out on the suddenly quiet sidewalk in front of the bar.

[FAINT SIREN]

Michelle stops, and thinking, she takes a deep breath and tries to figure her next move. Reily is getting harder and harder to hold up so she lets his hair go. He turns and looks at her for the first time. He is seriously intoxicated. They stand there for a moment, Reily looking at Michelle, and Michelle becoming aware of the sirens.

REILY
Take me with you. Please.

Michelle hears this, but doesn't even appear to think about it. She reverses the gun in her hand and then swinging it overhead with fluid tempo, she smashes Reily with it above the eye. He collapses as if his bones weren't there anymore; Michelle then runs across the street and jumps in the car. She slams the door and takes off with a quick screech of tires.

CUT TO:

[SIRENS ARE LOUDER]

Michelle's car hits the end of the street and takes a hard left.

CUT TO:
INT. CAR – NIGHT

Michelle drives with tears streaming down her face.

CUT TO:
INT. CAR – MIDMORNING

Shelley brings her hand out from beneath the seat. Still sitting in her car, she is crying now, silently.

CUT TO:
EXT. BOOKSTORE – MIDMORNING

Shelley's car sits still for another minute, she is vaguely visible but not identifiable through the car windows. The car starts and begins to head for the parking lot exit.

CUT TO:
INT. BOOKSTORE – MIDMORNING

Reily sitting still watching out the window sees the car drive away, he watches it carefully. The store is nearly empty now.

BOOKSTORE EMPLOYEE

Mr. Reily? I don't think we're going to get many more today.

> REILY

No, I don't suppose so.

They stare at each other for a minute. The bookstore employee becomes uncomfortable.

> BOOKSTORE EMPLOYEE

Are you working on something new?

> REILY

Yes, it's going to be a lyrical polemic about love and color, crime and happenstance, barbiturates and violence…

> BOOKSTORE EMPLOYEE

But… Isn't that what this one was about?

She indicates the small stack of copies of "Collision".

> REILY

Yes, but I don't think I got it quite right.

> BOOKSTORE EMPLOYEE

Oh. Well! I want to thank you for coming today, it's been a pleasure meeting you.

Reily fakes a small yawn, and in bringing his hand to his mouth tosses a couple of small pills in. He picks up his wine cup and shoots the rest down, with the pills, in one gulp.

REILY

My pleasure. Have a wonderful day.

He picks up his briefcase and walks out of the bookstore.

FADE TO BLACK

Praise for SEARCHER

Lovely, darkly funny poems, full of longing and sorrow but punctuated by crisp, dry wit and pitiless self-regard. If you have ever had to walk away from something beautiful and broken, Arbogast's moving, wry verse will school you on the worst-case scenarios you may have missed, and the grace notes that kept you there too long.

~ Ari McKee~Sexton

SEARCHER, Collected Poems 1988 ~ 2008
Available at lulu.com, amazon.com,
Or for signed copies, johnnyarbogast@gmail.com